Rowboat Watkins

# GO-GO GUYS

chronicle books · san francisco

We want to race around

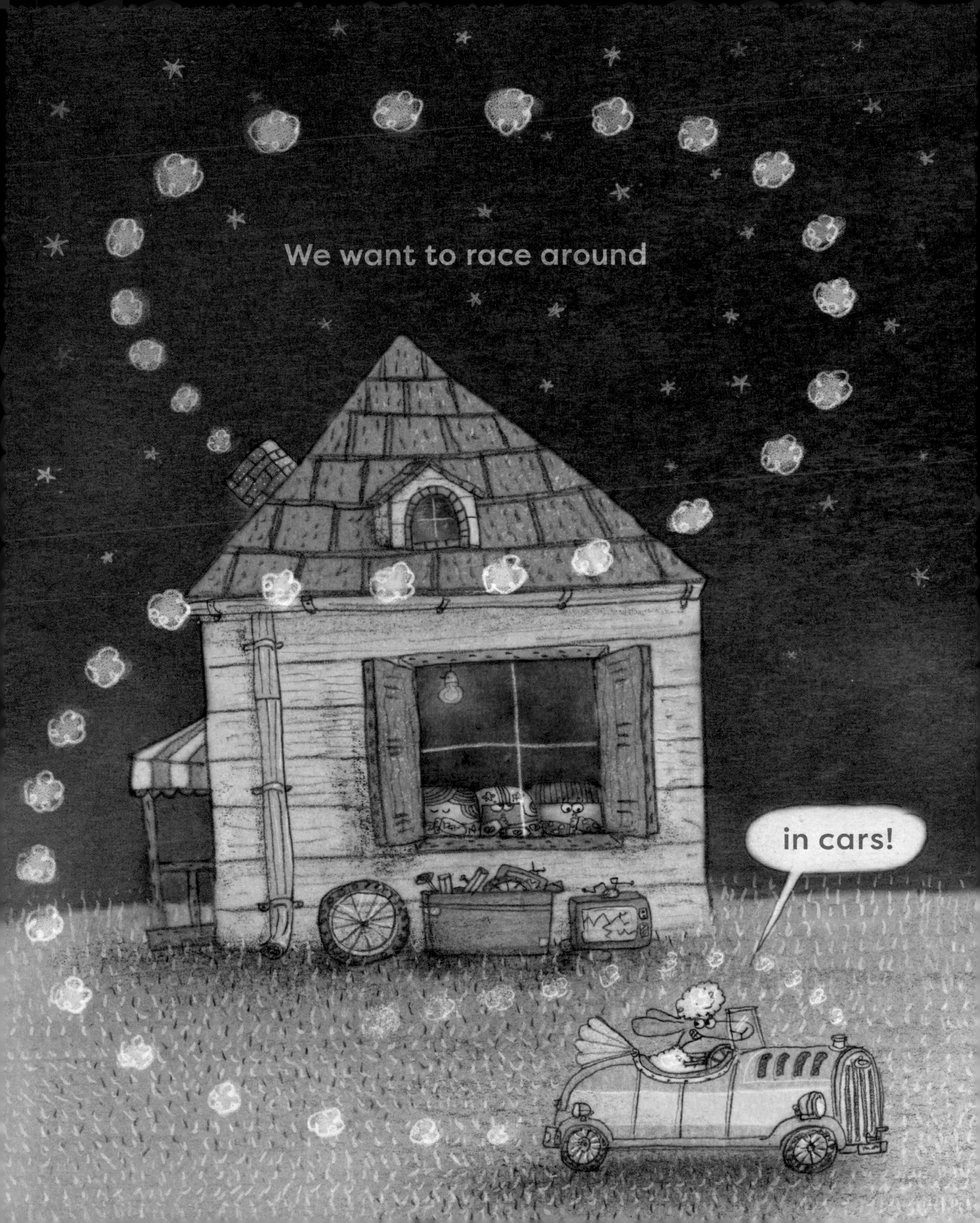

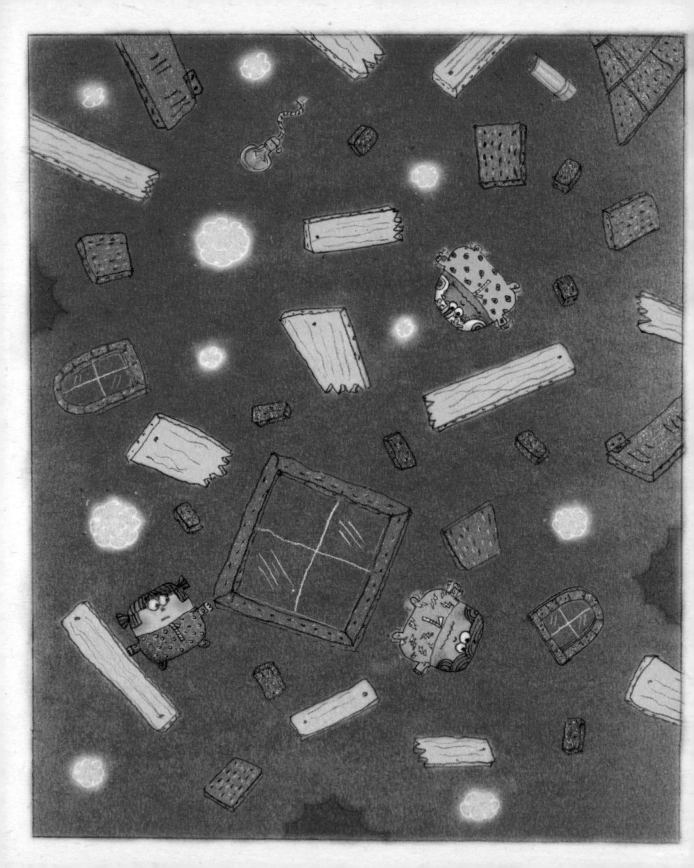

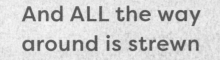

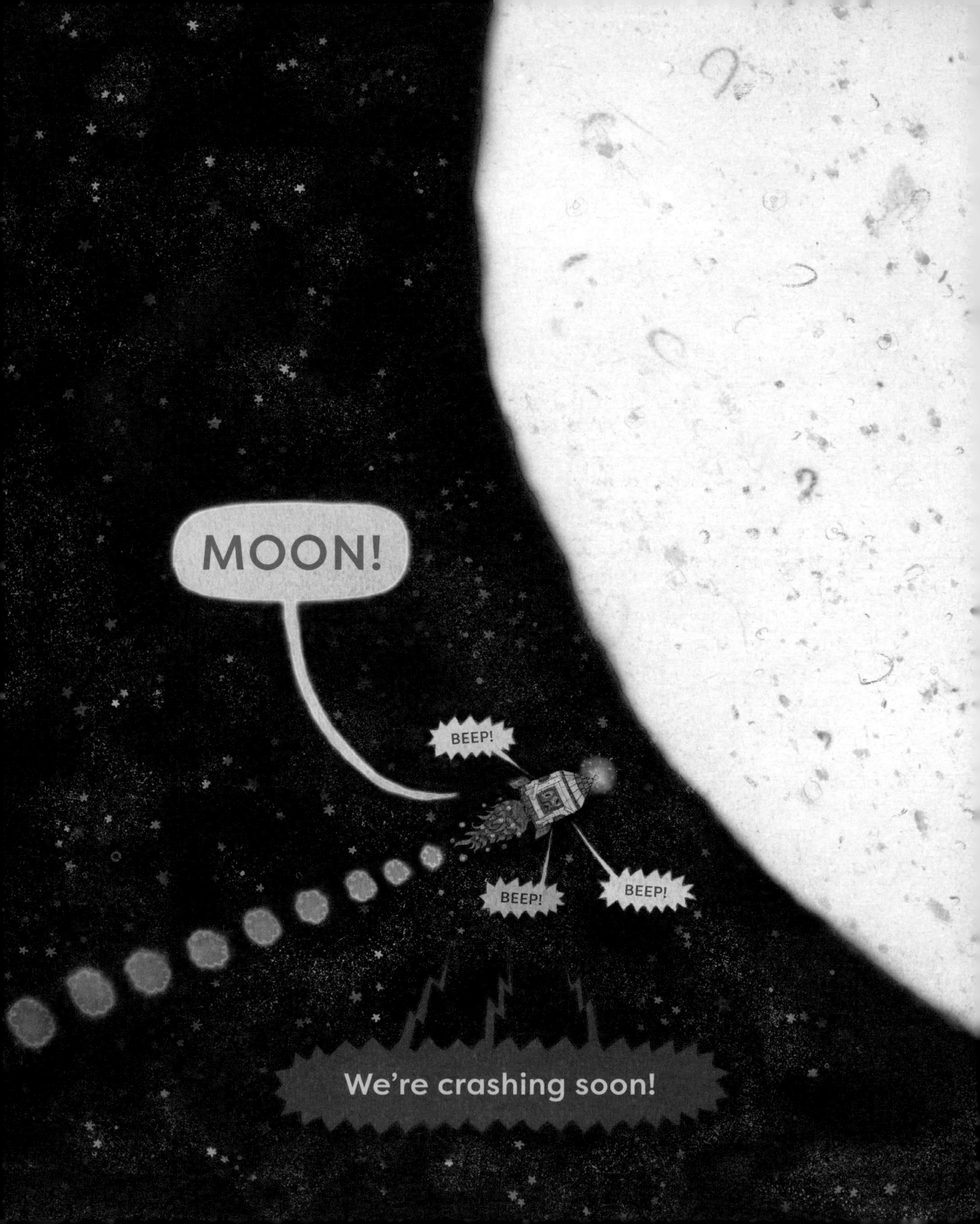
MOON!
BEEP!
BEEP!
BEEP!
We're crashing soon!

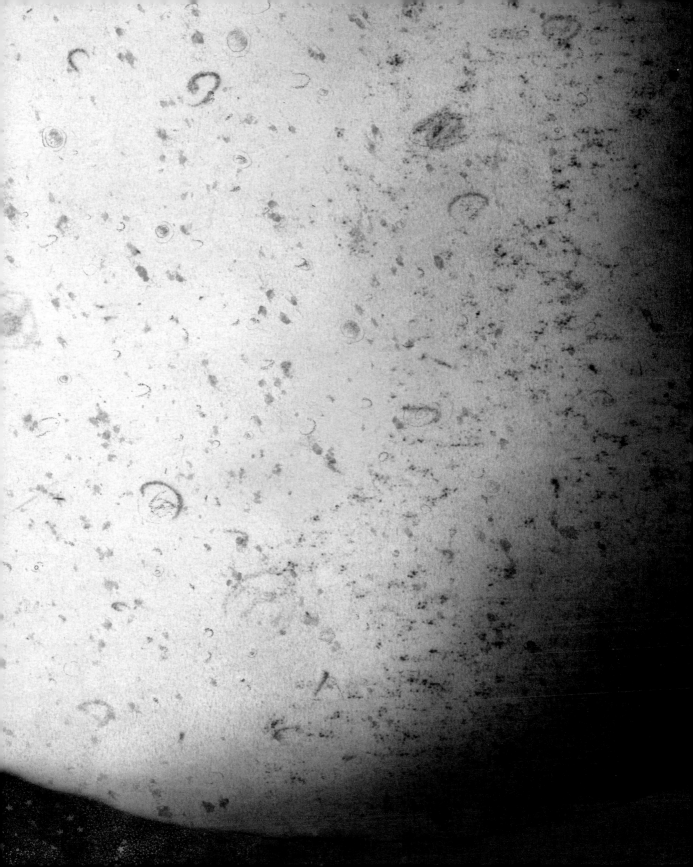

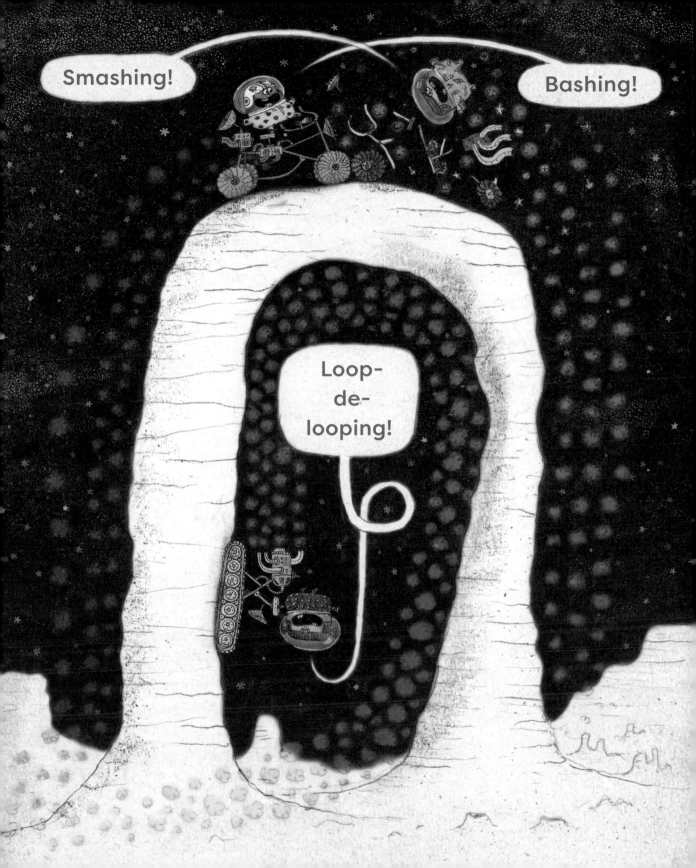

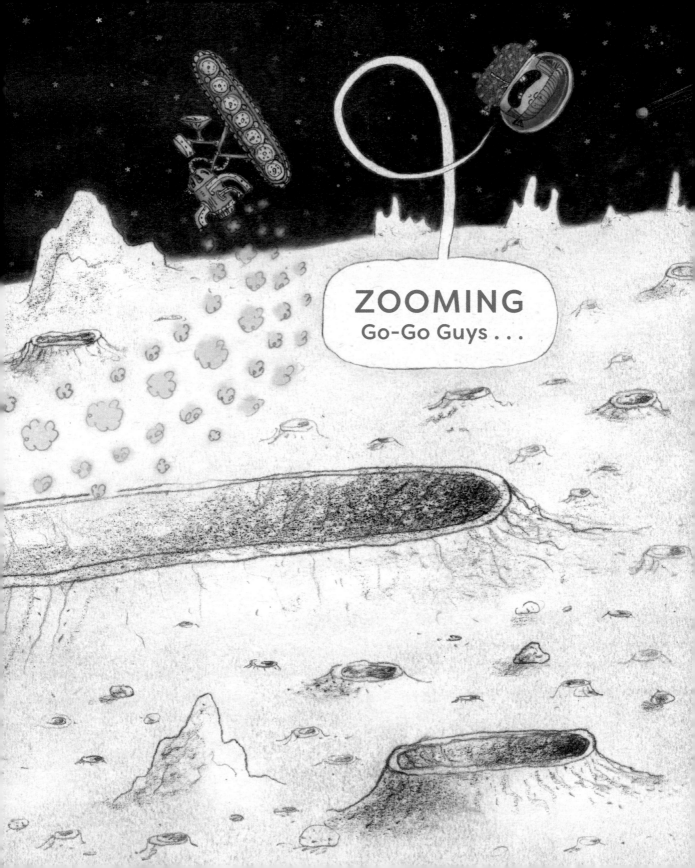

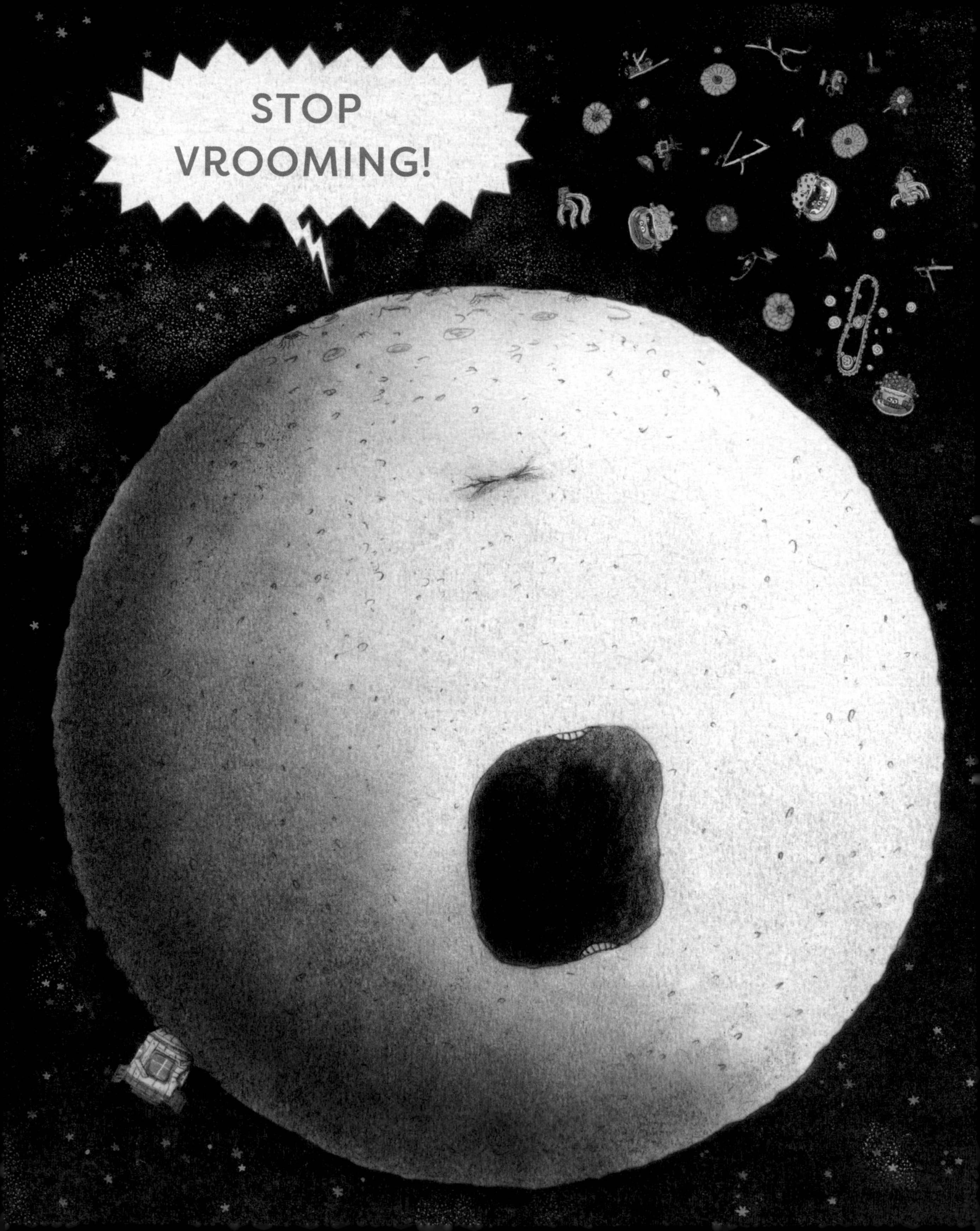
STOP VROOMING!

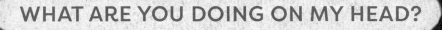

But Go-Go Guys aren't wired for sleep.
We're just not tired.
Our brains go BEEP!

for Caleb

Library of Congress Cataloging-in-Publication Data available.

ISBN 978-1-7972-0571-7

Manufactured in China.

FSC
www.fsc.org
MIX
Paper | Supporting
responsible forestry
FSC™ C136333

Design by Sara Gillingham Studio.
Handlettering by Rowboat Watkins. Typeset in Filson Pro.

10 9 8 7 6 5 4 3 2 1

Chronicle books and gifts are available at special quantity discounts to corporations, professional
associations, literacy programs, and other organizations. For details and discount information, please contact
our premiums department at corporatesales@chroniclebooks.com or at
1-800-759-0190.

Chronicle Books LLC
680 Second Street
San Francisco, California 94107

Chronicle Books—we see things differently.
Become part of our community at www.chroniclekids.com.